Wiff the Dragon

written by JUNE WOODMAN
and RITA GRAINGE

illustrated by
PETER KINGSTON

*This story has been adapted
for easy reading
and details are given
on the back endpaper.*

Titles in Series 815

Mr Noah's Animals:
The Lions and The Snake

Wiff the Dragon

Mr Noah's Animals:
The Monkeys and The Foxes

First edition

To the Rescue

Ladybird Books Loughborough

Wiff was a little green dragon. He lived in the woods with his Mum and Dad.

The dragons lived in a den. It was under two old trees.

One day, Wiff was playing with his ball.
He heard a big noise.

Wiff went to look.

Some men were cutting down the
trees. Wiff read a notice.
It said, "New Motorway."

Wiff watched the men.
Bang went the hammer.

Screech went the saw.

Crash went the trees, as they
fell down.

Wiff was afraid. He put his paws over
his ears. Then he ran away.

When it was dark, the men went home.
Then Wiff came back to see.

The trees had gone.
The dragons' den had gone.

"Where are my Mum and Dad?"
cried Wiff.

It was night time.
Wiff sat down and cried and cried.

The next day he said, "I must look for my Mum and Dad."

He looked in the woods . . .
but they were not there.

He looked round the farm . . .
but they weren't there.

He looked in the village . . .
but his Mum and Dad were not there.

There was a notice on the wall of a shop. Wiff read it.

"They have taken my Mum and Dad to the zoo!" he said.

It was a long way to the zoo.
Wiff flew.

Then he walked and then he flew a
bit more.

It was dark when Wiff got to the zoo.
The gates were locked.

So Wiff flew over the top of the gates.

THIS WAY TO
THE STRANGE
REPTILES

"Where shall I look?" said Wiff,
and then he saw a notice.

Wiff soon found his Mum and Dad.
They were in a big cage.

"Hello," said Wiff. He was happy to see his Mum and Dad.

"How can I get you out?" said Wiff. "I'll tell you what to do," said his Dad.

So Wiff flew and flew, back to the village. He was very tired.

He went to see the digging dragons.
Wiff told them about his Mum and Dad.

The digging dragons flew to the zoo
as fast as they could.

Dig, dig, dig went the digging dragons.

Then Wiff's Mum and Dad could get
out of the big cage.
They flew away as fast as they could.

On the way home they saw Wiff.
He was very, very tired.

Wiff's Mum flew down and picked him
up. "Thank you, Wiff," she said.

Then Wiff and his Mum and Dad
all flew away.

The Secret
Weapon

The dogs from the village liked to play in the woods.

They had lots of fun.
The dogs chased the rabbit.

They chased the squirrel.

One day they saw Wiff, the little green dragon.

Now the dogs chased Wiff.

"Help!" cried Wiff, and he hid behind
an old tree.

Wiff could hear the dogs.
"What can I do?" he said.

Then he saw some conkers.

The dogs came. **Sniff! Sniff!** They could smell Wiff but they could not see him.

A conker hit one of the dogs on its head.

Then lots and lots of conkers came down. The dogs ran away.

Wiff had been up in the tree.
He had dropped conkers on the dogs.

Wiff laughed at the dogs and came
down from the top of the tree.

The next day, Wiff was picking
blackberries.

The sharp thorns had cut his paws.

Wiff put his paws into the cool water.
Then he heard a noise.

The dogs were coming to chase him again. "Where can I hide?" said Wiff.

Wiff jumped into the water.

When the dogs came they could smell
Wiff but they could not see him.

Sniff! Sniff! Sniff! "Where is Wiff?"

"Where did that dragon go?" said the dogs, and they ran away.

Wiff laughed at the dogs and he peeped
out from his hiding place.

But one day, when Wiff was at the
farm, the dogs came again.

Wiff didn't hear them and this time
he could not run away.

The dogs growled and they showed
their teeth.

"What can I do?" cried Wiff.
"I must use my secret weapon."

Wiff puffed and puffed.
Soon he made a lot of smoke.

Now the dogs were afraid.

Wiff puffed and puffed and puffed.

Then big, red, dragon flames came out of Wiff's nose.

The dogs ran away as fast as they could.

Wiff laughed. ''I don't think I'll see the dogs again!'' he said.

Then he put his head in the cool water
because his nose was very hot.

Notes to parents and teachers

This series of books is designed for children who have begun to read and who need, and will enjoy, wider reading at a supplementary level.

The stories are based on Key Words up to *Level 5c* of the Ladybird Key Words Reading Scheme.

Extra words and words beyond that level are listed below.

Words which the child will meet at *Level 6* are listed separately, in case the parent or teacher wishes to give extra attention to these words and use this series as a bridge between reading levels.

Although based on Key Words, these books are ideal as supplementary reading material for use with any other reading scheme. The high picture content gives visual clues to words which may be unfamiliar and the consistent repetition of new words will give confidence to the reader.

Words used at Level 6

green	lived	old
day	when	time
next	round	zoo
tell	very	been
hot	because	